MUSIC FOR DOGS

First published in 2008 by
The Dedalus Press
13 Moyclare Road
Baldoyle
Dublin 13
Ireland

www.dedaluspress.com

Editor: Pat Boran

ISBN 978 1 904556 96 1 (paper)
ISBN 978 1 904556 95 4 (bound)

Dedalus Press titles are represented in North America
by Syracuse University Press, Inc., 621 Skytop Road,
Suite 110, Syracuse, New York 13244, and in the UK by
Central Books, 99 Wallis Road, London E9 5LN

Cover image © iStockphoto.com/Anna Bryukhanova

The Dedalus Press receives financial assistance from
An Chomhairle Ealaíon / The Arts Council, Ireland

MUSIC FOR DOGS

Work for Radio

Paula Meehan

DEDALUS PRESS
DUBLIN, IRELAND

ACKNOWLEDGEMENTS

My thanks to Kevin Reynolds, Series Producer of RTÉ Radio Drama, and to Lorelei Harris, Editor of Arts, Features, Drama and Documentaries, RTÉ Radio 1.

My thanks too to Shelly and Wayne Doyle for all their help.

The Lover received the 2005 Phonographic Performance Ireland Award for Drama.

In Memory

Paula McCarthy

1957—2001

Contents

Janey Mack is Going to Die

Janey Mack is Going to Die
was first broadcast on RTÉ Radio 1
November 19th 2001
as part of *All Talk*, a series of dramatic monologues.
It was produced by Eithne Hand.

Jane McDonald was played by Ruth McCabe.

JANEY MACK IS GOING TO DIE

A woman sits by the sea with a tape recorder.

There. Just there where the stones are. I'll start with stones and waves. That sucking noise—reminder of first breath, first suck. The insuck of the mother, the outsuck of the tide.

She pushes button. Tape turning over: sound of waves sucking through stones, a gull's cry, a dog's bark.

Testing one two three testing one two. Right.

Throat clearing.

By the time you both get this, Anne and Patrick, I'll be dead. It'll probably be winter, the heart of winter. Here now it is a poor enough summer's day. A midsummer's day. The beach is deserted and ... No.

Silence and littoral sounds.

Dear sister and brother, you'll have been given a copy of this tape by my solicitor, Harold McGee, of McGee McGonagle and McGregor—I kid you not. GeeBag as he's familiarly known to the junkie fraternity and sorority .... feck it.

She presses Stop. Presses Rewind.

Okay here we go again.

She presses Play and we hear sounds of waves sucking through stones, a gull's cry, a dog's bark. She presses Stop.

I'll take it from there.

Copies of this tape along with my last will and testament will be lodged with my solicitor Harry McGee whom you may remember from when he got me off that time I was caught coming into Rosslare with the five keys of Nepalese all those years ago.

By the time you get this, Annie and Padser, I'll be dead and you'll both be rich. Not filthy rich, mind, but richer than you'd ever dreamed, I bet. I was going to leave letters, but you, Padser, I'm convinced, are functionally illiterate. Or so I'd have thought seeing as you never replied back in 1996 when Julian OD'd and I wrote to you for help and I thought my world was ending. My world did end; but it's not the time and place and I should add in case you're feeling smug, Annie, that you also behaved abysmally then. And since. And before.

In fact if it weren't for two small occurrences from our collective childhood I'd not even bother getting in touch. But you are brother and sister to me and though you really did wash your hands of me bigtime—I can't resist this final irony. It must be clear ... No. I want you both to be clear about how much I despise you, your children, your petit bourgeois aspirations and all the delirium of your patios and your wall-to-walls and your ... I can still see your face, Annie, in the kitchen telling me how well your Robert did in his Leaving Cert and how fabulously (that's the word you used) he was getting on as an assistant manager in PriceValu and what a lovely girlfriend he had. While my beautiful boy lay stretched on the coroner's slab.

And you, Padser. Scumbag was written (tattooed in neon as Gerry Caulfield would say) in your eyes when you looked at me, Padser. Your baby sister. Of course you always thought I was a bit of a bike. Whatever about that—being a bike with a dead bastard seventeen-year-old druggy son splashed all over the *Herald* was another kettle of fish.

Where was I?

As I said there are two small incidents from the sad country of our childhood which redeem you now in memory.

Did I say I'm on the Burrow Beach? Burrow Beach. The best spot in the entire known universe. Nanny Mac would bring us here—out on the train—do you remember? She called it the Hole in the Wall. And then when you were old enough you'd bring us, Padser. You were like a bloody dictator. We used do Heil Hitler goosesteps up the beach behind your back. But you taught me to float. The summer I was seven. 1962. Before that I'd be terrified to take my feet off the bottom. But you came down into the water and took my head in your thirteen-year-old hands and talked me into lying back into them. The cold of the water in my hair, the sun warm on my face, your boy's hands under my skull and you talking soothingly, murmuring. For ages. And then your hands weren't there and I nearly panicked and *I'm here. I'll catch you.* And I didn't panic and I was floating.

And the Special Memory, tra-la, I have of you, Annie Moynihan nee McDonald! Or Annie Mickey Moynihan as you are commonly known, behind your back *loike.* Just as your beloved husband Michael is known as No Mickey Moynihan and reputedly likes it up the ass from renters in the Park.

Fuck it. I can't say that. No matter what. Fuck it. Poor Julian. Poor baby. My lovely son.

She stops machine. Lights up joint. Sucks in. Holds breath. Again. Sound of waves nearby being sucked into stones. And breath again deeply taken. And held. And let go. Until it is the exact same rhythm as the sea. Insistent barking starts up in background. Then she lets a big whistle —

Here, Whiskey. Leave that dog alone. Here girl. Good girl. Creatch. Creatch.

She rewinds to

... murmuring. For ages. And then your hands weren't there and I nearly panicked and *I'm here. I'll catch you.* And I didn't panic and I was floating.

Now where ... ? Yes. You, Annie. There's a story about you too attached to this beach. Padser had brought us two and the Doyle gang out for the day. Swinish, I'd say, was the technical term for him. He was heading here on his ownio with Lily Doyle; Ma & Mrs Doyle sicced all of us on them. You must have been about five, Annie. The famine was on in Biafra. Every night on the TV—starving black kids.

We got to the beach and dispersed leaving Padser to moon eye and grope the Doyle young one. We gravitated back around lunchtime for the sandwiches and MiWadi. The two big sliced white pans of jam sandwiches.

No sandwiches. No MiWadi. Padser came into his own. The interrogation. The tears. *I'll fucken burst-ya. I'll burst-ya.* And how eventually you cracked, Annie, and admitted giving them to The Biafran Family down the rocky end of the beach. And how The Biafran Family seemed genuinely bewildered when I was "sent" to get the grub back—I sure as hell didn't volunteer to go get it. They were probably medical students or something. They certainly looked well fed.

Anyway. Those two things. Incidents. Floating, The Biafrans. Let these two incidents be or stand for ... something ... Goodness? They've stayed in my memory all these years. Something to carry. Something to hold to.

I said I'd leave you both rich. You probably imagined me languishing in abject poverty out here since Julian died. You never darkened the door.

I suppose I should explain where I made the money. Not, as I bet was your first thought, from drugs. Go on! It was; wasn't it? Or even peddling me hole. Sorry. Sorry. Forgot how delicate you both are—peddling *my* hole. In fact nothing illegal at all. I merely became, in the current jargon, an entrepreneur.

Isn't that right, girl? See even Whiskey here at my feet recognises it. In fact Whiskey could be said to be the inspiration and guiding spirit behind the whole enterprise.

I'll go back to the beginning. Hardly three years ago. It was after dinner. Gerry had scored a dynamite bit of blow. You might remember Gerry from Julian's funeral. He was the very shook eighteen-year-old who woke up beside Julian's poor dead body. In that kip of a flat up the psycho end of the North Circular Road. All over the papers then. His family didn't want to know him—he was a country lad. In Julian's class in the College. Wanted to be an architect.

They were only kids. They were only messing.

Ah fuck it. I swore I wouldn't cry. Not in front of you.

Sniffs, nose blowing and a couple of deep breaths.

Anyway I took him in. Gerry Caulfield. To live with me.

REM we were listening to on a brand new CD player, well one previous owner who probably didn't even realise he was previous yet. It was very very hot. As was the brand new Apple computer, with Laser printer and scanner and manuals and a bloody lot of those little styrofoam yokes they use in packing. Now what are they called? Gerry knew the name. In fact that's exactly what he was telling me—the proper word for them—when I got the idea.

Gerry had been in the house for over a year at that stage. It was a link, do you see, to Julian. Kind of like Julian's ghost life unwinding as Gerry lived out his life. I don't know what I mean. I loved having him there. Though I sometimes got worried he'd end up adrift like myself maybe—especially with the robbing. He only ever robbed rich fuckers but. Of course the neighbours all thought it was kinky sex stuff. I was on the freeze list for a while. But fair play—Harmony Avenue adapts. Who can afford to call the kettle black? Look at the Kino Sullivan. Half the week in number 17 with Jo and the boys and the rest of the time next door in number 19 with Alice and the twins. The gas thing was there was never anything between us like that. He'd bring home his girlfriends and boyfriends and do whatever he wanted with them. Mind you, once inside his room (actually your old room, Annie).

The most I was getting was the odd throw-back when an old squeeze turned up. Which was enough. Which is enough. Is plenty. I've long reached the age when I've given up pretending to be stupid. And most men want you to. Pretend. They're more comfortable that way. Even the educated ones. They're the worst. And once you stop pretending, well ... you open your mouth and you don't know what's going to come out. Or which of your feet you're going to put in it.

Where was I? Feet ... Gerry ... the computer ... REM. Little did we know it then but soon there'd be no more need for robbing. It was a bit of a celebration—though there was nothing in particular to celebrate. We were just unaccountably happy. Almost as if we knew in our bones that our fortunes were changing. Our fates unfolding. And we'd both been having a hard time, financially *loike*. We were broke. But the summer was coming in, we'd enough draw for a few days and Michael Stipe was belting it out: "I said it all. I didn't say enough. That's me in the spotlight, losing my religion." I noticed Whiskey. She had her whole body right against the cupboard the speakers were resting on. We'd the bass turned way up. And her tail was going like billy-o. She was really grooving. Gerry made a cup of tea then and I started riffing on about Music for Dogs. That there was a market out there to exploit.

Whiskey's getting on, of course. A wee black and white mongrel with a bit of a collie in her. Julian bought her from the knackers with his Confirmation money. God love him. They saw him coming. But she's a terrific dog. Fertile in her day. Loved the ride. On Harmony Avenue alone there was Brandy, Champers, there's Gin in number 4 (Tonic's around on the Road), there's Harpic, there's Stag—he's only three legs. Who else? The Brennans I think called their one Harvey. That got run over by the Parish minibus. There was a Wallbanger on the Grove, come to think of it.

I don't know at what point it all got serious. I was telling Gerry about the Pet Rock phenomenon in the U.S. Remember the ads? No watering. No feeding. No walking. It just sits there where you put it. Pet Rocks: the low-maintenance pets.

And I was on about *Music for Dogs*. Recording on CD tunes that dogs would like. We were putting together a list of songs—and instrumental tracks. Gerry reckoned they'd love hip hop. Discussing half jokingly chasing up copyrights. Skitting about putting sounds on disc that only dogs would hear. High out of the human range of hearing, sounds that would get the dog excited. Then thinking about recording studio time. And research. And the money we'd need to acquire the rights. And the business stuff was starting to do our heads in. It would cost way too much to set up. Forget it.

Then I had it. What do dogs really respond to? Huh? The human vibe of their owners. It's the way you talk to them. The special dog voice you put on that gets them really going. Wagging the tail, wagging the whole shagging hindquarters with delight. It's the tone of voice of the master, or mistress. So what does it matter what's on the CD? It's not the dogs who are putting their hands in their pockets and pulling out the loot. Dog owners are the target. That's who we're selling to. Fuck the dogs. Once that hit us, the rest fell into place.

All we had to do was put a few sounds on a blank CD—maybe a whistle getting higher and higher in pitch until it goes out of range of human hearing. And then nothing. The rest of the CD would be blank. It'd be the owner saying things like "There, there's a good Rover. Do you like that, Rover? Aren't you the great boy?" That would get the dog going for sure. It'd be the master's voice that the dog would respond to. Wagging and smiling. Oh yes. Dogs do smile. Sure as soon as Whiskey hears my voice she's on her back waiting for her belly to be scratched. And it would only be people who really loved their dogs who would go out and spend €14.99 on a CD called *Music for Dogs*. In fact they'd have to be fucking crazy about their dogs. And that's exactly what we'd put in our ads:

Dog Lovers!
Are You Crazy About Your Dog?

Get Music for Dogs!
The Ultimate Treat for the Canine of Discernment.

I was dubious about that last line. But Gerry was attached to it and he reckoned it gave the CD a ring of scientific exactitude. I didn't think scientific exactitude was going to be a priority with our target consumer group. But as the business gurus say—the good manager is sensitive to the needs of her staff. And Gerry was already calling me Boss. Yo, Boss.

We got up sometime the next afternoon. I put an ad in *Hot Press* and the *Catholic Weekly*. Over the phone. Invoice me, I says. Jane McDonald, 'Music for Dogs', Gula House, 9 Harmony Avenue, Dublin 13. I chose the name Gula on the spur of the moment. I didn't want people thinking it was just your ordinary semi-d, and was leafing through one of Julian's old books on Ancient Babylon when I came across the little known fact—little known around here anyway—that the Babylonian Fate Goddess's symbol was a dog. So hula bula gula, we were flying.

Gerry went out and was back that afternoon with what he called a CD burner and fifty blank CDs. We designated the boxroom the workroom and Gerry set the computer equipment up. We didn't have a shilling but in some newfound surge of confidence, not to mention the very good blow, I got

21

tea, skins and cigarettes. For Gerry I got a jar of instant decaf and a packet of Kimberly biscuits. All on the slate over in the shop. Oul Pooly was so flabbergasted at the cheek of it that she just gave the stuff to me.

I designed the covers. We were going to use His Master's Voice, you know the dog listening to the horn—Gerry reckoned that'd be a trade mark. But just the week before I'd come across a page of a newspaper from the fifties—it was an inner lining under the brown paper lining in one of the drawers in the tallboy I keep under the stairs. The one that was in Ma and Da's room when we were kids. It was a drawing of a glamorous housewife polishing a hi-fi system with a wee dog at her feet wagging up at her. Gerry put up an internet site over the next few days too—music-for-dogs.com. Then I kind of forgot about the whole thing. The dope ran out and I came down and it was back to basics.

The first couple of letters enclosing cheques arrived a week later. Just two. One from a man called Andy Broe in Roscommon who had a sheepdog that had lost her foot in a chainsaw accident.

And one from a Mary Gibney in Knocklyon who'd lost her Jack Russell a year before and still wasn't over it and thought *Music for Dogs* would make her feel closer in spirit to Jay Orr.

I didn't know whether to laugh or cry. But Gerry and meself sat down at the kitchen table and parceled up the CDs with a note telling Mary and Jack that we were sorry for their troubles etc. Also telling them that their human ears would not be able to actually hear *Music for Dogs* as it was pitched way beyond the human ability to hear. Only dogs, coyotes and wolves could "hear" it. There are quotation marks around the "hear" by the way. We didn't want any legal comebacks.

This was because the CD burner was acting up and we couldn't manage to record anything onto the discs. We cashed the cheques up in The Comet and we drank the money. Sure it was a month before we actually set up a bank account.

We treated the whole thing as a laugh ...

Mobile phone rings.

Feck. Hang on now.

She turns recorder off.

Ger. Hello. Ah sweetheart, how are you? Hmm. It's very early for them to want to know that, isn't it? What about *Christmas Music for Dogs?* Or *Seasonal Favourites for Dogs?* We don't want to push any religious buttons. You think the word Christmas doesn't only imply Christians?

Laughs.

Ah that's very good, Ger. We'll go with that. Who cares whether they get it. *Adeste Fido.* Ah yes. It's too good to ... I'm great. Not a bother. I'll see you later, Gerry.

Now. Let me see.

She turns back on the recorder.

To cut a very long and twisty story short, not to beat about the bush, and to cut to the chase; *Music for Dogs* took off. Mega.

Whiskey's after swimming over the first channel and is chasing up and down after a heron on the sandbank.

She whistles Whiskey back.

He-re girl. Whiskey! Come on, girl. There's another heron just standing still in the shallows. It is so beautiful here. Mysterious in the mist. Hardly a sinner on the beach.

Okay. Okay. The Business Starter Unit. I'll take it from there. It was the order from Los Angeles that really boosted us. The website had been up only a few weeks and Dogs'R'Friends, a big dog food and dog accessory shop in LA put in an order for 5,000 CDs. I mean we were still on first name terms with most of our customers. Gerry even had a date with Natasha and her Alsatian from Glenageary, and believe me Gerry was not the dating kind. And we half felt we were doing something illegal. The LA order threw us into a state of paralysis. We drank pots of tea, rolled non-stop joints and hardly left the kitchen for four days. Somehow a phonecall got made. Somehow the next Monday morning myself and Gerry were waltzing the length and breadth of a Starter Unit up on the industrial estate. Somehow I'm on the floor of the Starter Unit painting Gula Enterprises in gold on a purple slate to hang up discreetly on the railings. We decided to be discreet. We decided to be very discreet.

That was a happy time. Growing the business. Seemingly that was what we were doing. That's what the experts call it. We were just having fun. We'd four of the local kids and a couple of old guys and Lil who came in to make tea and clean and generally be like a mother to us all. She'd cook up a lunch every day too which was a big help all round—gave a stability to the place. We had a good system going. Relaxed. But when a rush was on everyone would rally round and it'd be all hands on deck till the rush was over. There was once we did three days non stop. Campbeds in the canteen.

I loved most the notion of packaging up this silence and sending it off to the four corners of the earth. All these little bundles of silence. I loved the idea of a person in a room with a dog listening hard, really hard, to nothing. I thought ... I still think ... there is too much noise in the world.

Within six months we'd outgrown the Starter Unit and had moved into the old ConEco Building and had a warehouse up the M50. We were, are indeed, phenomenal in Japan, so much so that we set up an outpost of the organisation there. Mitsuko, who I met in the Café Rouge one rainy Tuesday and took home with me, set up *Music for Dogs* in Kyoto and covers distribution in Asia. I believe there's interest from the Chinese—even though they've a seriously different take on the human-dog relationship.

We'd diversified of course—*Music for Dogs 2, Country Music for Dogs*—(dedicated to Andy Broe in Roscommon)—*Jazz for Dogs*, the surprise runaway hit—*Gospel for Dogs*. *Music for Puppies, Music for Bitches*, the specialist range—*Music for Terriers, for Retrievers, for Pointers, for Poodles* (a huge seller). We introduced a personalised service where you filled in your dog's name—*Music for Rex, Music for Genja, Music for Buttons*. There was one woman had a dog called Clitoris. I kid you not. A surprising hit was *Music for Watchdogs*. It was really big in Canada for some reason. Sold like hotcakes for two weeks and then just a dribble. I used feel it was like the weather—invisible currents moving through the atmosphere creating outbreaks here and there. It's unpredictable. It kept us on our toes. We laughed. We laughed till we cried.

We refused to talk to the media. Or rather befuddled them. Gerry would pretend to be Russian or the caretaker of the warehouse (you haven't lived until you've heard Leo from

Macroom talk to *The New York Times*). The maddest things were said about us. On one memorable day we were a front for both an extreme anti-globalization terrorist organisation and for the European Neo Nazi Movement. The more bad press we got, the higher the sales. Gerry had a huge graph covering one wall of the dispatch room. The week Bob Dylan called *Music for Lap Dogs* the epitome of contemporary pop the pin went off the top of the graph and four inches across the ceiling.

For one solid week we were all over RTÉ when they found out there was an Irish connection—they only twigged there was an Irish connection when we brought out *Ceol do Mhadraí*—

Screeches—hello Marian; hello Joe; hello Pat!

That's what I remember most from that mad first year: the laughs. Sometimes in the lulls— lulls being rarer and rarer— we'd skive off, Gerry and myself, and come down this beach. We'd often just nap that summer. Doze off for an hour in the sun. It was a beautiful summer. Sometimes on the edge of a doze Gerry would talk about Julian, about the life they had, things they got up to together. Sometimes really private stuff. It made me feel close to Julian. I don't think Gerry had any idea what he was doing—then again maybe he had—but it was the greatest gift I'd ever been given.

I had so little of him left to get close to. Do you see? I remember going into the flat a couple of days after he died and looking for traces of him. The landlord—a smarm who worked in the Financial Services Centre—rang and asked me to come and take his "effects" away. There are quotation marks around that "effects" by the way. Gerry told me later that Julian had been working off some back rent in blow jobs. See why I'm thankful to Gerry. See why I love him. Everyone else gave me back pious victim-images of my son. Gerry gave me

Julian the Wild in all his crazy bad boy days. Which he would have grown out of, which he would have survived.

There was precious little by way of "effects". A guitar he'd had since he was fourteen. The funny jumper that youngone who was in the art college made him. What was her name? A beautiful youngone. Six books. Four of them text books for his course. A Jamie Lee Burke I got him for his birthday and a book of Walks in the Southwest —seemingly himself and the youngone were going to some festival in Cork and planned on dropping acid and walking the ridge around Gougane Barra. We went there after—Gerry and myself and the youngone and put part of his ashes into the lake there. We put more of them into the sea here. I even put a pinch on the compost heap. Which I probably shouldn't be telling you. Do you see, I thought that everything in the garden that grew then would have a connection to him?

I've lost the thread again. I lost the plot a long time ago! Wasn't that what you said, Padser? I probably did lose the plot. I remember thinking when you said that—yes yes I want to lose the plot. Certainly if the pair of ye had found the plot, or knew the plot, or even were the hatchers of the plot then I sure as hell wanted to lose the fucking plot.

Of course neither of you have a clue I'm sick. It would never cross your minds. How long has it been since either of you asked me how I was? How I was managing? How I was getting on without Julian? Hmm? Enough said.

It's not that I'm bitter. I've had a fucking great life. And I can tell you this. The money means nothing. Oh *Music for Dogs* means an awful lot. The laughs alone ... but the money? Phit. In the wind. Like Julian's ashes. Like my own soon enough.

Okay. Okay. Back to business. You'll both be left comfortable. Don't come sniffing around for more. I mean that. The will is so tied up you'll lose every penny you have trying to fight it. And it was made before I got this morning's results. So it is not a decision made in haste but something I've thought out clearly.

Six months, the doctor said. Probably minimum. But not a lot longer. It'll be very fast at the end, and sure if it's dragging on, so to speak, I've a contingency plan. Does death drag on? Or out?

I've one memory of us united against the world in something like camaraderie. The summer we were sent to Ma's cousin out at the Naul? Old Róisín? Do you remember she left us to clean out the henhouse while she took a lift into Balbriggan for the messages? What age were we? I was six, I think. First time I'd seen a live chicken. And do you remember after we'd swept out all the soiled straw and scrubbed down the boxes and perches with Jeyes Fluid and put the lovely fresh golden straw back in and, Annie, you had the brilliant idea that we'd go one better and give all the chickens and hens a bubble bath and shampoo. And do you remember how proud we were of how clean and fragrant everything was? And do you remember Róisín's face when we told her what we'd done? And how we were expecting to be praised to high heaven? And how this horrible look came over her face? And how she punched you, Padser, in the face, like she was a man? Do you remember the hands on her? And how over a couple of days the chickens began to die off in twos and threes? Everytime you went out there'd be another few gone. You see, we'd washed all the oil out of their lovely shiny feathers. They must have got chicken flu or pneumonia. And do you remember how we got up in the middle of the next night and snuck out of there?

The grass was wet. I remember we were stung to bits by nettles cutting down through the back field to the road. And there we were like the children in the fairy tale trying to figure our way back home through the night landscape of North County Dublin. But we did it. And we never said a word to Ma. And we never mentioned the dead chickens again.

Jesus. What the waves of the mind cast up. Like these things here left by the outgoing tide. A bit of a polystyrene float, a shoe, maybe a dead sailor's shoe, a Fairy Liquid bottle. Plastic bags of blue and pink tangled up in sea weed. A child's burst ball.

Silence. The sound of waves lapping. She stops tape. She rewinds. Presses Play.

… the waves of the mind cast up. Like these things here left by the outgoing tide. A bit of a polystyrene float, a shoe, maybe a dead sailor's shoe, a Fairy Liquid bottle. Plastic bags of blue and pink tangled up in sea weed. A child's burst ball.

She laughs. Presses Record.

Goodbye, Annie. Goodbye, Padser.

She turns off machine.

Whiskey. Whiskey. [*She whistles.*] He-re Whiskey. Come on, girl. Come on. Good girl. Who's the best girl?

— The End —

The Lover

The Lover
was first broadcast on RTÉ Radio 1
January 18th 2005.
as part of
The Seven Ages, a series of plays.
It was produced by Daniel Reardon.

Sinta McGrath was played by Lisa Lamb.

"And then the lover,
Sighing like a furnace, with a woeful ballad
Made to his mistress' eyebrow."

—*As You Like It,* William Shakespeare

THE LOVER

We hear Nick Drake's 'Black Eyed Dog', medium volume at first. Then higher. Then higher. Door opening. Real blare. Until—

He's on the bloody Nick Drake again. Dad. Dad. Dad! Will you turn it down? I'm trying to study. That's the fifth time he's played it. It's graven into my head.

Sound of door slamming. Nick Drake low in background.

He's worse than a teenager. And *he* gets on *my* case. Now. Dee di dee. Pen. Paper. Okay here goes—

Dear Mam.
No, no. Dear Estelle. No. Definitely not. That sounds wrong. I never called her Estelle when she was alive. Star Ma. Karma. Okay.

Dear Mam,
The counsellor ... No. My counsellor, Ivor Hogan, my bereavement counsellor actually, said I should have a go at writing you a letter. No. That's not it either. How the hell do you start?

Dear Mam,

I've been attending counselling since your suicide and Ivor Hogan, the very nice man who counsels me, said I should write you a letter regularly and tell you how I'm feeling about things. No one need ever read the letters but they'd be a way of expressing my grief. I can tear them up or burn them when I've finished. Or I could keep them as a kind of—what did he say? —a kind of emotional diary. A soul diary. Ivor talks like that.

That sounds ridiculous. All I know is you are a lump in my throat. When I think of you. A pain under my heart. I keep holding my left breast like the pain is physically there. Bloody hell.

Sound of page being torn up.

Okay. Again. Now.

Dear Mam,

Bulletin from the living. From this side of the great divide. I fell in love last week. With a boy called John. He has green eyes and curly brown hair. I wish he was here with me now and us curled up in the bed. I love the smell of him. He's written me a poem. I'm not sure what it means exactly. He compares my eyelashes to the waterweeds at the foot of the bridge.

That sounds even more ridiculous. If I could only get started. How do you write to the dead anyway? Do you pretend they are still alive and up to speed with what's going on in your life? Ivor says I can set the terms myself. That it's really myself I'm writing to and what matters is the expression of what's on my mind.

I only really have the one thing on my mind. More John. More John. More John. I'm sore from last night. I can hardly write that to Mam. Even if she's dead. Dear Mam, He fucked me good. I'm sick for the want of him. When I think about him something turns over in my stomach. Or my womb. See that's the crux of the matter. I'd never say things like that to my mother. Okay. One more go.

John Lennon singing 'O my love for the first time in my life ...'
Sinta opens door again and shouts—

Dad, Dad please. I'm trying to study.

The smell of ganja would blow your head off. No wonder he sits listening to that miserable music all day. All songs sung by dead people. *That's* where I should start.

Dear Mam,
Since you so thoughtfully topped yourself, Dad is going quietly round the twist. He sits in the front room listening to dead singer-songwriters especially those who died young. Janis Joplin, the Buckleys (father *and* son), Sandy Denny, Nick Drake. If he's not in the front room he's out in the shed. Counting nails or something. Who knows? He smokes South African weed all the time. He hasn't been in work since you ... went. He had compassionate leave at first and now he's on sick benefit. Mr Taylor called around and I just know by his attitude that Dad probably doesn't really have a job to go back to. He's moved out of your room into the spare room in the extension, which looks like a bomb hit it. He's on a campbed there like a dosser, like he's camping in the house.

Owen passed his eleventh birthday in a kind of catatonic trance. You know the way he worries because his birthday falls on Stephen's Day? In case he won't get his quota of birthday presents as well as Santa Christmas presents. But all Christmas has come to mean to us is your present, Mam. That was some birthday present, Ma. Some Christmas present. A Christmas Box. Right in the guts. Oh yeah. A box. A punch. A blow.

Stop. You see, Ma. It ain't easy. When I go in to tuck Owen up for the night his face is a puddle of tears. He blames himself. Fuck it, we all blame ourselves. I hope Dad hasn't woken him.

You knew he'd find you. He'd be in first from school. He'd find you there dead in the bed.

No. No. No. I'm sorry. No blame. No anger. 'O my love for the first time in my life my eyes are wide open. O my love for the first time in my life my eyes can see. I see the wind and I see the trees. Everything is clear to me now.' Dad plays it over and over. Over and over. Do you hear it? Do you? Wherever you are.

Sound of Sinta weeping.

Okay. Get a grip. One more start. Ivor said if I was stuck just to look out the window, describe what I saw and take it from there.

Dear Mam,
It's nearly one o'clock in the morning here in the land of the living. There's a full moon shining over the green and most of the lights are out now in Harmony Park. Barney from number 12 and Mac from number 17 are camped in Doyle's driveway. Fido Doyle is in heat again. You can hear her howling and whimpering with desire when you pass the house. At least I assume it's desire, for who can know the mind of a dog?

Dad's below listening to sounds from his youth. From both your youths. Owen is fast asleep. I looked in on him a while

40

ago. He has Teddy back again. I don't know where he dug him out of. I was sure he'd gone in the bin with the soother. Anyway. You wouldn't even know it was a Teddy. One eye, no arms, no ears.

Dad bought him a leopard gecko for Christmas. It was Ivor's idea really. He said the responsibility might help. Having something to look after. I think he meant a puppy, but Dad, I'd say stoned out of his head, got talked into buying the lizard in the pet shop. Three hundred euro altogether: what with the glass thing he lives in—it is an aquarium actually, only you don't put any water in it—his heat mat and thermostat which takes up half the kitchen, and all his toys. Special tree bark to lurk under. Special lighting. He's a nocturnal guy. And artificial vegetation that approximates his natural habitat. Or so it says on the packet.

In fact the same leopard gecko, Iggy, is responsible for me falling in love. I had gone into town for its special food—crickets. They're sold in egg-boxes. Iggy has to have live food. Crickets, which Owen sprinkles with this kind of nutritional supplement powder. I call it flavour enhancer. Sometimes little frozen mice, pinkies, that we warm up on the radiator. They look really weird. Hairless.

It was on the half-five bus. That I met him. John. It was a miserable wet February day and I barely caught it. I was soaked to the skin but at least I got a seat upstairs. The bus crawled along. It was hot and steamy. There was a couple behind speaking … Russian maybe. Eastern European. They were having one of those controlled arguments, their voices low and intense. I must have fallen asleep. I felt a tug on my arm. Excuse me! Excuse me! I woke up looking into the most beautiful set of eyes on the planet. Green. So unbelievably green I thought a whole new word should be coined for it. Really. I felt like I was falling into them—down down down through a forest canopy of green. Everything stopped. I swear. The bus was stopped anyway—in a traffic jam. 'Your egg-box is singing.' They were his first words to me. 'Your egg-box is singing.'

Of course what had happened was the pet shop had given me singing crickets. You can specify, you know—silent or singing. You would not believe Mam how much I've learned about geckos—their foodchain, their habitat, their cute little ways, since you opted out. An unexpected by-product of the grieving process. It's a pity it's not on the Leaving Cert. Ah fuck.

No. I'm sorry. I'm getting angry again. Normal says Ivor. That's his favourite word—normal. Seemingly all this is perfectly normal.

Anyway, there I was on the bus falling into John's green eyes though I didn't know his name was John or that before the night was out I'd be deflowered. Now that's a word you don't hear much anymore, Ma.

This letter has gone off track, dear Mother. What was I on about? The crickets, the bus, John. Yes John, 'Your egg-box is singing.' And he was right. There was the absolute silence of the bus stopped in traffic and singing its little heart out, a cricket. Everyone listening to it. Here, Mam. I'm sending the sound to you now. Through the veil that is between the living and the dead. Between your world and my world. Can you hear it?

The sound of a cricket singing.

That was the sound I fell in love to. Hear it again, Mam.

Cricket singing again.

The bus pulled off and I dragged my eyes away from the youngfellow beside me whose name I didn't even know yet. I looked out through the condensation on the window pane, and where a rivulet had washed a clear space I saw that I'd gotten on the wrong bloody bus. The 29 instead of the 29A. Which means, as you know—okay, as you once knew, with human consciousness, when you were alive—that it doesn't go into Harmony but past the estate and up the main road. It's a fifteen-minute walk back. And it was lashing. I think I said this to Green Eyes. There was a lot of fluster and John rang the bell. Insistently. The bus actually stopped. John shouted down the stairs to the driver. 'Emergency! Stop! A girl is sick!' I stood up and the bottom fell out of the paper bag I had the messages in. It had disintegrated with all the wetness on the floor. There were apples and oranges. They went all over the place and everyone was scrabbling under their seats. John gathered them in the front of his hoody, and the next thing I know we are standing at the side of the road in kinks. We just couldn't stop. And the rain was lashing into us. Then he just kissed me in the rain.

It was bitter cold and the rain was nearly knocking us off our feet. I could smell oranges from his hands.

He walked back with me to the house. There was nobody in. Owen had a swimming class and was going back to Shane's for his dinner. There was a note from Da on the table. 'Gone to see a man about a dog. Back late.' And a fifty euro note under the candle. That could mean anything. He was off on the piss. Or gone to score some grass.

43

I felt suddenly shy. I didn't even know this guy's name. And here we were taking off our soaking clothes up at the hot press and wrapping ourselves in the good blue towels. Everything was suddenly different. Even the taste of myself. Like a chemical reaction or something. Everything has a kind of shimmer around the edges. And there was the smell of oranges.

My hair, as you well know—Did I ever stop moaning about it? —goes frizzy when it's wet. What did John say? 'You have the most beautiful hair I've ever seen. It's like burnished gold. Or beaten bronze.'

I still didn't know his name. Then. I was tongue-tied. I didn't have a clue what the words meant until that moment. Tongue-tied. There was nothing to be said.

He lifted me up and carried me into your room. I was going to explain but then it felt okay. He pulled back the covers on the bed and tucked me up in it. When I write it down like this it feels like a desecration. 'And your mother not even cold in her grave,' Dad would say, in fact does say a lot these days, when he wants to lay it on with a trowel.

God, I can't put that down in a letter to my mother. Like a confessional. So.

Dear Mam, I'll draw a discreet veil over what happened next. Here's the rain drumming on the extension roof instead and pouring down the gutters.

Sound of rain drumming, pouring, gurgling.

The rain stopped. A huge quiet came over the house and I fell asleep. John—I finally knew his name!—was shaking me awake.

'Shh. There's someone come in,' he whispered. It was Owen. I could hear the fridge door slamming closed. Then the tv in the front room and various channels being surfed. He settled on a station. Loud. I could make out the voices of the mechanics from *Pimp my Ride* on MTV.

Me and John dressed like thieves in the night. Crept down the stairs. I was hoping I could sneak him out without Owen noticing. Oh no. Not a chance. Big Ears.

'What were you doing up there?' says Owen. And he's scanning us with the eagle eyes. Scan. Scan. Scan. He knows well. 'Studying.' 'Yeah, Right.' And the first actual leer, an actual technical leer, comes over Owen's face. 'Does Da know *he's* here?'

Talk about being saved by the bell—Shane rings in for him and he just grabs his jacket and runs. He's halfway down the garden and he turns and he gives me this mad grin and then starts fondling his crotch and gyrating his hips. Then Shane and him jump over the wall and head away over to Shane's gaff. Oops. Sorry, Mam, I know you hated that word. 'This is not a gaff—it's a home.' As you hated, come to think of it, the word kip, as in sleep. You'd shudder if Da said he was going for a kip. You hated the bed being called the scratcher.

But I'm no psychologist. As we know. As you were always telling me—'Cut the amateur psychology.' I had the answers to everything.

You'd sit down there at the kitchen table in your dressing gown and light up. And we were always leaving you in it. In the stew of your life. The broth of your life. We went out the door every morning and left you in it. DART money, bus fare, loan of ten euro, lunch money, money for a copybook, money for mobile

45

credit, money for the toll, new this, new that, new the other. Hands out. Gimme. Gimme. Gimme.

I never thought of after, and what you did when the house was yours again.

I've lost track now, Mam. Where was I?

Sound of Sinta thumbing through pages.

Here it is. Dah di dee. Dee dee. Yes. Owen and Shane ran off. Me and John keyed in each others' mobile numbers and he headed out across the green. He looked so beautiful. He is so beautiful. I can't tell you. I can't even begin. I stayed at the door till the very last glimpse that could be caught. And then I was at the window upstairs—even after he'd turned the corner I watched for ages.

I got a text. I texted back. The mobile became like an extension to my hand. We were on to each other all the time. And I mean all the time. All that first night.

I heard Da come in at about three in the morning. I knew by the sounds he was making that he was drunk. He knew he was drunk though and was doing everything with exaggerated care.

The next morning was nuts. Da was sick as a parrot. Owen had gone back into the numb zone. I don't know where he goes when he goes in there but there's no reaching him.

He was first off out of the house. I knew not to even look at Da. Then I left.

I'll never know what tipped him off. I left your bedroom really neat. I changed the sheets. Maybe I put a different kind of sheet back on. Maybe Dad smelled testosterone around the place. Like in this documentary I saw the other night. About wolves. If Dad is the Alpha Male of our little pack then he'd smell a challenge a mile off. Who knows? Owen swears he said nothing.

But when I got in from school there was a change in the house.

I came in the back door and was heading upstairs to shower and get out as quick as I could to go meet John at Sutton Cross. We were going to go for a walk. Mam! At this very minute I thought I heard your voice in my ear. You know your sarcastic voice. *Walk. Walk. Sinta McGrath discovers the use of her legs, folks!*

I'm wandering off again. Where was I? Yes.

Dad was standing very tensely by the door of the front room. 'Sinta, could I have a word?' I followed him in. He stood in front of the stove and I sat in the red chair. He was kind of dressed up. He'd put on the dark blue cord jacket. The one he's worn to every single parent-teacher meeting. My heart sank. I figured I was in for it.

'Sinta. I don't want you to, well not that I don't want you to, I don't think you should—call me Dad anymore.'

'I'll strangle Owen'—was my first thought.

'You're becoming a young woman. A young lady, indeed. From now on I think you should call me Christopher. Or Chris, if you like. I think it'll mark the end of our childish, I mean

47

childhood, father-daughter, parent-child, type relationship.'
What could I say? He went on 'And the start of a more, well,
grown up phase.'

He knew nothing, I thought. Thank god. It was just normal.
As he said, father-daughter stuff. Coincidental, sure, that it
happened the day after my deflowering; but a coincidence
none the less, I figured. I was so relieved at being off the hook
that I was totally unprepared for what came next. It took me a
few beats to catch up with what was going on.

He whipped a packet of condoms from his jacket pocket, took
out one, tore the foil, fished out the condom, blew into it, blew
gently into it, actually. Then with the condom in one hand held
by the little blip on the top of it, he grabbed a sweeping brush
from up against the wall and proceeded to show me how to roll
the condom onto the top of the sweeping brush.

'I hope you got all that,' he said. 'In this day and age you have
to be careful.' Then he put the rest of the packet of condoms
down on the sofa and marched out with the brush up on his
shoulder.

John didn't laugh when I told him all that. He started to cry.
Can you believe it? We were up the Rhodies. If it wasn't pissing
down we'd have been looking out over the whole of Dublin.
The alleged view, he called it. Do you remember we had a
picnic up there for my sixteenth? You can't imagine, Mam,
how completely different every single thing is in our lives now.
Or maybe you can. Can you?

Anyway it was getting dark. And he asked about you. 'You
never mention a mother,' he said. Like a statement—not a
question. I didn't tell him you'd killed yourself, Mam. I'm not
sure how to say it yet. I heard a man on the radio talking about

how his wife had 'committed suicide'. Like it was a crime and I know back in history it was. I know a lot more about suicide than I ever thought I'd need to know. And lizards, of course. I just told John that you got very sick and died. He never *actually* asks questions. Or if he does they're always asked in a way that gives you an option not to answer them. If you know what I mean. Not like an interrogation.

So. Yeah. I told him you were sick and you died. We were in under a huge rhododendron and it was real dry in there. The rain made everything smell lovely. John's skin. So smooth. He has these freckles over his nose. Listen to me. But every single thing about him was just so beautiful. Is just so beautiful.

I took John home to meet Dad today after school.

Sound of Sandy Denny singing the first verse of 'Who knows where the time goes ...'

Will you listen to that now. He's back on Sandy Denny again. That was your favourite song.

Sinta joins in humming, eventually singing as Sandy Denny's voice fades until it is just Sinta's voice singing:

Across the evening sky
All the birds are leaving
But how can they know
It's time for them to go

Before the winter fire
I will still be dreaming
I have no thought of time
For who knows where the time goes?
Who knows where the time goes?

But, Mam, it's nearly spring. Actually it's officially spring. Saint Brigid's Day has been and gone. Owen made a cross in school and it's up now over Iggy's aquarium, though there's no water in it. I think I explained all that to you. There are even daffs coming out along the motorway.

Yeah. John met Dad today. We came in just as he was finishing off cooking a pasta thing. His face was red and sweaty and he'd the big pot over the sink transferring the pasta into the colander. I think he was going to dish it up—there were a couple of plates on the table and Owen was sorting out Iggy's grub. Dad asked John if he wanted some. He did. Then Dad put the pasta in with the sauce, put the grated cheddar on top and stuck it in the oven to brown.

I can just hear you again, Mam. Your sarcastic voice— *Christopher McGrath cooking dinner.*

We all stood there awkwardly watching Iggy chase his dinner around his, eh, habitat. He had just shed his skin so he was chewing on that too. I didn't know what to say. Neither did anyone else and the silence dragged on and on. I was beginning to feel the beginning of a giggling fit bubbling up. I looked at Owen and we both lost it. We were snorting and snuffling and choking. There was no holding it in. We were in hysterics. Dad was beaming at John. I think he fell instantly in love with him too. Like in that old song you both love, loved, where the Lord's daughter brings home Willie of Winsbury to meet her father, and even though Willie is a commoner and the love affair is doomed, the Lord—or is it the King? maybe he's the king and the daughter is the princess—anyway, she brings Willie home and the father claps eyes on his beauty and says—

If I were a woman as I am a man
your bedfellow I would have been.

Is that how the song goes?

Sinta sings:

The king he has been a poor prisoner
a prisoner long in Spain
And Willie O the Winsbury
has lain lang with his daughter at hame

I think the King has him hanged in the end.

We all ate the pasta and John knew loads of cool stuff from the
web about geckos and singing crickets. Their importance in
Chinese culture. Stuff about fighting crickets too. Did you
know that in China they put a kind of resin on the cricket's
legs to make it sing sweeter. Though it mightn't be such a good
idea to get into the personalities of crickets when you're
watching them being hunted to the death every night live in
your own kitchen.

And Dad was really happy that Owen was out of the numb
zone—even for a little bit. And maybe he was happy for me
too that I was out of my numb zone. Though I caught a few
old wolf sniffs.

There. The sounds are off. That means Dad has gone to sleep
at last. When John left we found his hat stuck down the side
of the armchair. 'Planning to come back for it, is he?' said Dad.
I'm running out of stuff to tell you, Mam. And I don't want to
get all mushy. My hand is tired. Worn out.

I've just had a text from John. He has an essay due tomorrow. That's something we have in common. Last-minute merchants.

I'd love to post this to you. Take a stamp from the book in the olive bowl on the shelf, where they're still kept, Mam. Walk out now across the green and through the sleeping estate down to the main road and post it in the box at Reilly's wall. Or I could walk on down to the sea and tear it up into flitters and toss it to the waves.

I've to see the counsellor tomorrow. Ivor. Hogan. I think I told you his name. He specializes in traumatic bereavement. Not that all bereavement isn't traumatic. But he does the seriously heavy stuff. Murder and stuff. Violent death. I'd love to ask him more about the murder stuff but you kind of just know not to. He asked me to do this letter thing and I put it off of course to the very last minute. I get off school for the morning to go see him. And if I'm not up to going in for the afternoon, that's cool. Sometimes I just have to come home and go to bed.

Yes, I've written to my dead mother. Yes, it got stuff off my chest. Yes, it got easier as I got going. But Mam, I won't be showing the letter to him or anything. And he knows nothing about John. And me falling in love and losing my virginity. Imagine. He knows none of it. So maybe I'll say nothing and see does he notice anything. Or see how long I can keep it to myself. A secret. Because when you talk about things it can feel like you are giving them away. And it is impossible anyway to tell anyone what anything is really like. And I am afraid that if I talk about John and love I'll cheapen them and start to change it all, so in a few visits time it'll be like talking about something that never happened to people who never existed.

And now.

Now I think I'm going to stop.

Your loving and forgiving daughter,

Sinta

— The End —

Threehander

Threehander
was first broadcast on RTÉ Radio 1
October 23rd 2005
in *The Sunday Playhouse* series.
It was produced by Cathryn Brennan
and sound supervision was by Richard McCullough.

The Mother was played by Ruth McCabe.
The Father was played by Garrett Keogh.
The Daughter was played by Laura Murphy.

THREEHANDER

Sound throughout of respirator and medical equipment. The sound is regular, rhythmic, always in background, low down in sound mix, but more audible during silences in the room. It gives the effect of a kind of ur-breathing and is used to punctuate movements in the script.

Different accoustic for the daughter's voice. She can hear the parents but they cannot know that she is hearing them.

We hear 'Dimming of the Day' sung by Richard and Linda Thompson.

MOTHER

I think that's enough.

Sound of radio being turned off.

I love that song but it's too dreary. Just at the minute.

Sound of rhythmic pulse of respirator and medical equipment.

Look at you now. The picture of peace. You'd swear you were just asleep. You look like you're just dreaming.

I still can't believe you did it. I keep expecting you to jump up off that bed and shout—April Fool, I'm only kidding!

That game when you were a child? You'd pretend to be dead. And we'd stand there talking about you: Oh she's dead, we'd say. Stone dead. We'll have to dig a big hole in the ground and bury her. You look for the shovel, I'd say to your Da, and he'd be like—Oh I'll have to go to the coffin shop and buy a coffin.

It was that time Sooty died. We thought it was your way of coping.

You'd jump up then and shout— April Fool, I'm only kidding! No matter what time of the year it was.

DAUGHTER
Give over, Ma. It wasn't like that at all. Nothing to do with the cat. You've forgotten the rows. It was a way of stopping the rows. I'd lie on the floor in the kitchen and I'd hold my breath, and when one of you noticed me you'd play the game. But sometimes you didn't notice me. I'd lie there for ages.

MOTHER
You look so peaceful. Not a line on your face. I wish you'd open your eyes. I can hardly remember what colour your eyes are.

DAUGHTER
Hazel.

MOTHER

Blue, I think. Deep blue. I'll never forget the moment I looked in your eyes after you were born. It was so … so …

DAUGHTER

Sentimental?

MOTHER

… so … so….

DAUGHTER

Sick?

MOTHER

… so powerful.

DAUGHTER

Wow.

MOTHER

Like I was truly connected in a deep, a very deep way to the universe. You were such a precious gift.

DAUGHTER

How can I shut her up?

MOTHER

There's so much I never told you. About my life. And now that you are …

DAUGHTER

Go on, Ma. Find the word.

MOTHER

… you are … dead really.

DAUGHTER

Ah now here. Wait a minute.

MOTHER

Dead to us. Unreachable. I wouldn't say that to your father of course. If you ask me, he's all too ready to give up on you. I can read him like a book still. After .... seventeen ... eighteen ...

DAUGHTER

Twenty years apart.

MOTHER

... Do you know it's twenty years? I can still read his mind. He won't say it but I know he believes you're not coming back from this. You poor creature. Someone has to believe in you. And I do.

DAUGHTER

That's frightening. That is truly frightening. My mother believes in me. Ha bleeding ha.

MOTHER

What's the time? He should be well back by now. The traffic is mad out there. A bus crashed into the Luas.

Look at your lovely feet. Will I give them a rub? Is that nice? Do you like that? You look so calm. I wish I knew what's going on in there. In your poor head.

DAUGHTER

I'd prefer to know the time. Is it morning? Afternoon? I'm a coma detective. Piecing it all together from the snippets.

Are you touching my feet? I can hear a kind of chafing but I can't be sure. If I could only send a signal out. Wiggle a toe. But no matter how hard I try ...

MOTHER

I was so proud of you. I am so proud of you. Am proud. Am.

I went into labour at my twenty-first birthday party. In front
of everyone. Before the party even got going. I was so
embarrassed. Mortified. Your father was locked. He didn't
realise what was happening. Neither did I really. I didn't think
I was so far gone. None of the families even knew. You were
early too. A little scrap with your face all scrunched up like a
boxer. The hands going like billy-o. A fighter, I said, as soon as
I looked at you. You couldn't wait to get here.

DAUGHTER

Couldn't wait to get away when I found out what the gaff was
like. Planet earth? Surely some mistake? Was that it?

MOTHER

You were such a happy child.

DAUGHTER

No I wasn't. I lived in a state of perpetual fear.

MOTHER

And you brought us such deep deep joy.

DAUGHTER

Pull the other one. For Jaysus sake. I remember you hated
motherhood. You beat me black and blue on a regular basis. I
swear I was punch drunk most of my childhood.

Sound of match being struck but not catching. Twice.
Then it catches.

She's after lighting a cigarette. I hope she blows it over me.

MOTHER

You were our pride and joy. Your Da doted on you, even when our relationship was falling apart.

DAUGHTER

All I remember was Da out every night at union meetings. Saving the working class. I thought he was going to save me. But I was only a little girl, not a class. Sorry! Not *the* class. That's what he called it. The class. Like everyone knew. Holding forth. Saving the class. Mostly from itself. He couldn't save me. Oh he'd the fine speeches. But not for me. He couldn't string two words together. After you left home he'd look at me sometimes like I was from another species. He's scratch his head and give me a few bob.

He hated being on his own with me. Mrs Duff would come in and mind me after school sometimes. When she was between jobs on the sewing. She'd sit at the kitchen table and do hems while I ate my dinner. Miles of hems. Then she'd clean up and go back next door. She never said much to me. Which was amazing—considering she was the Harmony Avenue Public Broadcasting Corporation.

Sometimes he moved in a bimbo—that's what I called them, though to be fair they were usually very bright youngones, but who wants to be fair when you're lying there in the dark listening to your Da fucking next door, before you even have that word for what they're doing. Most didn't last long anyway when they discovered I was part of the deal.

I read every book in the house—from Mills and Boon to Reminiscences of the Cuban Revolutionary War. I thought they could save me. They did for a while.

MOTHER

I've always been very proud of you. I want you to know that. I was so proud when you became a teacher. My daughter the secondary school teacher. I know it sounds corny, like something out of a movie. But I'd actually go round trying to work it into conversations. Oh—give me some of that nice brocolli: my daughter loves brocolli—she's a secondary school teacher by the way.

DAUGHTER

Pathetic alright. You never said anything to me. Jesus you didn't even keep in touch. I'd hear on the grapevine you were living in Cork or Bristol or up the Welsh mountains with a wind generator.

Sound of door opening. Enter FATHER.

FATHER

Do you know who I'm after meeting downstairs? Joey Kilbride. Remember Joey? The Wheatmills Strike. That was some strike. Eight months the lads were out. Winter too. There was nothing in the strike fund. But they stuck it out. You just don't get that kind of spirit now.

How is she? No change?

MOTHER

No.

FATHER

You were smoking.

MOTHER

Sherlock Holmes.

FATHER

They'll go mad. I wouldn't blame you.

DAUGHTER

Ah go on. Do.

FATHER

I was in the flower shop down at the entrance and I got these big flowers she liked. Likes. Likes. Sunflowers.

DAUGHTER

It was the painting I liked.

FATHER

Joey's in to visit the mother.

MOTHER

What? What?

FATHER

He was telling me a terrible story about a chap he knew whose youngone was in a coma for three months. Never came out of it. Terrible. Terrible business.

MOTHER

What?

FATHER

Everyone you meet has a coma story.

MOTHER

Whose youngone?

FATHER

Nothing to be done.

Do you remember Joey? And his lad Saoirse?

MOTHER

Joey? Saoirse? Yes. Yes. Of course I do.

DAUGHTER:

No you don't. You were gone by then, Ma. I remember him though. Marches. We'd always meet Saoirse at marches. I used love to see him coming. Both Das'd relax. It meant we'd be able to bunk off to Burgerland. As long as we checked in at the usual haunts. The GPO first. Then O'Connell Bridge just to show willing. They'd be more relaxed about us and we'd see them up at the Dáil in about an hour. Two if there were a lot of big nob speeches, or Christy Moore.

Don't forget your shovel if ya want to dig a grave.

The trick was to get them relaxed.

MOTHER

Was he the lad with the red hair?

FATHER

Joey?

DAUGHTER

His hair was golden. Like an angel he was. Cherubic. We had to beat them off in Mr Quirky's. The pervert who offered Saoirse the fiver for 'Licky-ficky'.

MOTHER

No, his youngfellow. I said was he the lad with the red hair?
Was his mother Yvonne?

FATHER

No. No. She was an Englishwoman. Big. Stout.

MOTHER

Are you sure it wasn't Yvonne. From Clonmel.

FATHER

Jesus—will you shut up about it.

DAUGHTER

Steady. Steady.

MOTHER

I only wanted to place him.

DAUGHTER

It was a long, long place ago. Last time I saw Saoirse?
Girlfriend on his arm. Gorgeous looking youngone. Sweet
sixteen. It's that long. Ten years.

MOTHER

What happened to the girl in the coma?

FATHER

A car. Speeding. She was a passenger. She was thrown clear.
Not a mark on her. Just the neck broken.

MOTHER

I think that'd be easier.

FATHER

What are you on about?

MOTHER

A random act. Act of God they call it. An accident.

FATHER

Yes. It would. Maybe. I don't know. Maybe it would be easier to bear. Suicide leaves a terrible legacy... legacy ...

MOTHER

To those left behind.

Sound of FATHER weeping.

I'm sorry. Here's a hanky.

FATHER

I'm alright. I'm sorry.

MOTHER

Go on. They're free.

FATHER

Thanks. Thanks. I think I could cope with her death better than this waiting. The twilight zone. God forgive me I thought today for the first time that she'd be better off dead.

DAUGHTER

Well I'd sure love to oblige. Isn't that where we all came in? Much as I am ... relieved? ... gratified? ... by my father crying. There is still a suspicion that it's another attempt to get at me. Underneath it all. Am I paranoid? Am I fuck!

Dry your tears, Da. They only make me feel guilty. Guilty that I didn't die in a car crash or walk under a bus. Can you believe it? I ask myself. I'm the one after committing suicide and I'm supposed to feel guilty. Like not only am I a failure in my life, but I can't even manage to kill myself. Oh ineptitude. A total failure. A failed suicide. I wonder if they have that on my chart. Failed suicide. FS coma.

FATHER
I've been trying to ring Anja and let her know the score. I can't get her on the mobile.

MOTHER
Puts a whole new meaning on *up the pole.*

FATHER
She's Slovene: Anja is Slovene.

MOTHER
Carry on up the Slovak.

FATHER
That's the drink talking.

DAUGHTER
Hell. This demonic comedy. Forever trapped here unto all eternity listening to the Ma and the Da acting out the same old, same old.

Or unto that moment when they pull the plug. Was it ever otherwise?

MOTHER
Me? Drink? I didn't get a chance. Down the drain. You poured it down that plughole. You're a miserable fuck. Did you think

I was going to drink the bottle at my own daughter's sickbed? That was to have for emergencies.

DAUGHTER
I'd plug my ears if I could move.

FATHER
You won't even talk about it.

MOTHER
Talk about what? Your girlfriend?

FATHER
There may come a time when we have to talk about ... We may have to do the unthinkable. I'm putting it this bluntly even though it breaks my heart because it is the unthinkable but it's sitting like an elephant in the corner waving its trunk about and nobody's mentioning what the fuck is going to happen if the worse should come to the worse and someone has to think it out loud.

MOTHER
What are you saying?

FATHER
Sooner or later it's what we may have to decide. To pull the plug.

MOTHER
But ...

FATHER
But nothing. I want you to face up to it now. That's why I poured your drink down the drain. This is best handled sober.

DAUGHTER

Au contraire; sober she just couldn't handle it.

MOTHER

I asked you not to use those words. She's not an electrical appliance.

DAUGHTER

You turn me on, I'm a radio. I'm a country station. I'm a little bit corny. I'm wild for you ... Joni Mitchell. Singing. I wish I could sing. I wish I could utter a sound. Any sound. Like no amount of will can force the sound out. That time I tried to blow into a didgeridoo. Just couldn't get the sound. The fellow on Grafton Street let me have a go. Said he was an aboriginal himself.

MOTHER

Well, are you just going to stand there?

FATHER

I'm so tired.

DAUGHTER

The aboriginals themselves.

FATHER:

We need to face facts.

MOTHER

Facts.

FATHER

You heard what the doctors have been saying.

MOTHER

Hah.

DAUGHTER

What did the doctor say today?

MOTHER

What did the doctor say today?

DAUGHTER

Wow.

FATHER

You've heard him yourself. There's nothing new.

MOTHER

Today. I want to know. I should have been there.

DAUGHTER

Please, Ma. What did he say?

MOTHER

He thinks she's a vegetable. A turnip. Doesn't he? Admit it.

FATHER

To be fair to him he doesn't use those words.

MOTHER

No discernible brain activity.

DAUGHTER

I'm in here. I am in here. What's the use. I have to calm my
mind. I was right. I knew it. I knew O'Hagan was giving up
on me. The way he said it to the nurse. *Her beautiful hair.* Just

that offhand remark. Her beautiful hair. The last time he was in. When was that? Yesterday? I slept after. Or did I? Did I sleep or lapse back into a coma?

MOTHER

Doctors get it wrong. What about that woman who came out of a coma in Wyoming after eight years.

FATHER

The woman who said she'd been abducted by aliens.

MOTHER

That's beside the point. She was a nutcase. The point I'm making is they didn't just pull the plug after a few days. O'Hagan is too hasty, if you ask me; but who is asking me? Nobody's asking me.

FATHER

It's nearly a week.

DAUGHTER

A week? Is that all they're giving me?

MOTHER

I feel she's in there. I know she's in there.

FATHER

Nobody's saying anything at this stage.

MOTHER

You're trying to prepare me for something. Aren't you? I want the news. I don't want to be kept in the dark. What did O'Hagan say? I should have been there.

FATHER

Look—this is the news. This is the reality.

MOTHER

Over my dead body. I'm not going to abandon her now.

FATHER

You should have thought about that years ago. Abandonment.

MOTHER

That's below the belt.

FATHER

I'm sorry.

DAUGHTER

No, you're not.

MOTHER

At least she's stable. There's been no change. No deterioration.

FATHER

Stable? She's in a coma. There's been no brain ... fuck. I give up.

DAUGHTER

Brain what? Brain waves? Is that what they call them? It feels like such an old-fashioned word. Dahling, I've had such a frightfully good brainwave.

Brainstorm. Brain box. Brains to burn. According to the monitors.

Coming to ... coming to this state which is best described as ... what? Suspended animation? Perhaps I really am as good as

75

dead already, brain dead, that is, as they say, and I am experiencing all this from the other side. I don't believe it though. I am in my body. I feel. I feel therefore I am.

But coming to—it was like swimming up through crude oil, something thick and viscous, like molasses. Coming to, or as come to as I am, like waking from the mother of all hangovers. But even with the worst hangover, the most mind-bending, mind-boggling trip, where the brain felt like it had been used as a football by a twenty-a-side team at closing time on the streets of, say, Tullamore, before they piled into the chipper. The brain felt shagged.

It won't follow orders, the body. The brain says, flutter an eyelid. Waggle a finger. Shift a leg. Elbow the nurse. Surely when she takes my pulse she can feel the willpower surging through my veins. If I could only get a signal over. Over what?

The divide. It was like swimming up through treacle only I could not break through to the light. To the sunlight.

Hard to know if it is day or night. Unless the folks are in and they mention it. Am I near a window? I feel nothing on my skin. The largest organ. You'd think I'd feel heat or coolness or sweat. Nothing. Yet I can hear. I can almost smell. The nurse earlier. She must have been wearing a strong chemical. She's from the Phillipines she told Ma. Maybe a perfume. I wanted to sneeze. Not smell then but definitely the physical sense of being in the presense of a strong chemical. Perfume. Or disinfectant.

If I could only send a signal. I am not dead. I am not dead.

MOTHER
She's not dead.

76

FATHER

She might as well be.

DAUGHTER

Don't give up on me. I can hear. As clear as a bell. The Buddhists say it's the last to go. Hearing. That as long as it's present there's a chance to be liberated from the wheel of suffering. Must be like an emergency act of contrition. *The Tibetan Book of the Dead.* That's what it was called. Subtitled: The Great Liberation Through Hearing in the Bardo. The Bardo. The between place. Yes, I'm in the Bardo.

Most compassionate holy book. If all else failed and you couldn't get liberated off the wheel of suffering, the book would give you advice at the very end for choosing an auspicious womb out of which to be reborn. I found that very funny at the time. And then frightening—the thought I might have chosen Ma's womb the last time round.

MOTHER

She had everything to live for. That's what I can't understand.

FATHER

We'll never understand.

MOTHER

We have to try.

FATHER

File under mystery.

MOTHER

Put her in the file with Irene, so.

DAUGHTER

I knew it was coming. I knew she'd bring up Irene. A small payback for the drink reference earlier.

FATHER

Irene has nothing to do with it.

MOTHER

There's never been a suicide in my family.

FATHER

Listen to yourself. Just listen.

Irene was like a mother to her.

MOTHER

Exactly.

FATHER

Suicide's not a contagious disease.

And I'm still not convinced Irene drowned herself.

MOTHER

It mightn't be a contagious disease but there are patterns.

FATHER

And what about you?

DAUGHTER

This should be good.

FATHER

Drinking. The way you drink. To oblivion. She's just as likely to inherit that gene. Isn't that what alcoholism is—a very slow suicide. Slow suicide and put every one else through the wringer too.

MOTHER

That's all that counselling talk. I've always taken a social drink.

DAUGHTER

You could sing that if you had a tune.

FATHER

You could sing that if you had a tune.

MOTHER

You know nothing about me. The life since I left you.

FATHER

I'm extrapolating.

MOTHER

Extrapolate away. I've always admitted I went through a rough patch. You'd drive a saint to drink.

FATHER

I drove you! I drove *you?*

DAUGHTER

Now we're motoring.

MOTHER

You should see yourself.

DAUGHTER

You should hear yourselves.

FATHER

I'm too old for this.

MOTHER

I never abandoned her. I was forced to go. I had no choice. You gave me no choice.

FATHER

You left. You walked out You didn't even have the courtesy to leave a note. At least she left a note.

DAUGHTER

I left two notes. Two suicide notes.

MOTHER

Just because I left didn't mean I didn't love her.

FATHER

Don't start. What about her Communion? Confirmation?

MOTHER

She didn't want to make her Confirmation.

FATHER

Don't twist things. You know what I mean. You were never there for her.

MOTHER

I was so.

FATHER

Go on then.

MOTHER

I did my best. I always tried to take her for a holiday.

FATHER

Four times. One. Two. Three. Four. In her entire life. Brilliant.

DAUGHTER

Wales. Remember Wales, Ma?

How old was I? Nine? No. Eight? Yes. It was my first time out of Ireland. We got the ferry. Watching the land recede. Is that Ireland? I asked. First time a sense of my own country.

You took me to The Atlantic Hotel in Aberystwyth. Right up the top of the building looking out over the sea. Our own bathroom and a big double bed. Afternoon tea and ornaments in all the shops and swimming and the Funhouse and then you nipped out for a message. You were going to get me a comic, you said.

You didn't come back that evening. I thought something had happened.

Then I knew nothing had happened. It was just you. The way you were. I must have fallen asleep eventually. I woke in the bathroom on the floor wrapped in an eiderdown. It was pitch black. No window. I was afraid.

When I looked in the bedroom there was the man from the Funhouse, from earlier in the day. He'd been taking the tickets at the door and then he came on in a big top hat with red sequins. He made jokes and introduced the acts. I didn't get any of the jokes but you laughed. I thought it was a bit sad. The lions all depressed looking.

I stayed in the bathroom and waited until he left. It took hours. I never let on I knew. And you did bring me back a comic—it was folded into a small square where you'd stuffed it into your purse.

FATHER

Ah for Jaysus sake. You're not lighting up another one.

Sound of mother weeping.

Ah here. Look, I'm sorry I shouted at you. Have your cigarette.

MOTHER

How could she do it?

FATHER

Nobody knows. She seemed okay. I mean up and down.

MOTHER

You should have let me know.

FATHER

You should have kept in touch. There was nothing to let you know.

MOTHER

People just don't suddenly take it into their heads to top themselves.

FATHER

We had no idea. She just seemed a bit down. She went to the doc. He examined her. He's in a terrible state too. He had no idea.

MOTHER

There must have been signs.

FATHER

I'm telling you there wasn't.

MOTHER

You don't have to be so defensive.

FATHER

I'm not defensive.

MOTHER

Well, you sound it.

FATHER

She went to the doctor. She said she was fine. She looked fine.

MOTHER

You should have told me.

FATHER

I didn't realize ... nobody could have realised. Just how bad she was. She looked fine.

MOTHER

I had to find out from a stranger. I only found out about my own daughter by accident.

FATHER

I was here. I was freaked. I hardly knew myself what was happening.

MOTHER

I should have been told immediately.

FATHER

I was going to phone when you arrived. I was trying to get a number for you.

MOTHER

That's what you say.

FATHER

That's the truth.

MOTHER

The truth.

DAUGHTER

I went to the doctor. Yes. I went to the doctor. I told him I was low. Feeling down. He asked me had I had a row with the boyfriend. Ha, ha, ha. No, I'm just low, weepy. Ah— premenstrual tension. No, this is all the time. How long? Two months? Six? I told him six. It could have been a year. It got really bad when I went back to school.

FATHER

She seemed okay. She was at home most of the summer. We were away a lot ourselves. We'd see her for a few days and then she'd be gone. Or we'd be gone.

MOTHER

I heard you bought a place.

FATHER

It's only a shack.

MOTHER

It's well for some.

FATHER

It's near Anja's folks.

MOTHER

In Poland.

FATHER

Jesus. Slovenia.

MOTHER

And that has nothing to do with her suicide.

FATHER

She got on great with Anja.

DAUGHTER

Theoretically I got on great with Anja. Like I'd nothing against the old man getting himself a child bride. She used say we were like sisters. We weren't. She was better looking than me for a start. She'd better clothes. She looked cooler. She was better educated.

FATHER

They were like sisters.

MOTHER

That must have been embarrassing. How old is Anja again?

FATHER

Has your informant not filled you in?

MOTHER

I have a number of sources of information. It's pathetic I have to rely on others to know what's going on with my own daughter. I hear it from an old neighbour.

FATHER

I bet it was Louise Duff ...

MOTHER

I hear from an old neighbour that you've moved in a mail order bride.

FATHER

Drop it.

MOTHER

Under our daughter's nose. Is it any wonder she went off the deep end?

FATHER

Ah now here, wait a minute.

MOTHER

I hear this from a neighbour and the next thing I hear our daughter is taking her own life.

DAUGHTER

Now who's got the moral high ground? Ding. Round four. Pretty evenly matched.

FATHER

I thought we agreed to let go of all this stuff.

DAUGHTER

Jettison it. Throw it overboard. Clear the decks. The air.

I'm tired now. He hasn't mentioned the meeting with O'Hagan. That's bad. Go on Ma. Ask him.

FATHER

I'm sorry. I don't know what to say. I got no sleep last night.

Now you can take that look off your face. Stop. I haven't been sleeping.

MOTHER

They say you need less as you get older.

DAUGHTER

Below the belt.

FATHER

The age difference made no difference to you. You were hardly twenty when we met.

MOTHER

And you were only gone thirty. It was nothing. I mean you're sixty now and how old is yer one? Twenty four? That's what I heard. Younger than your own daughter.

FATHER

This is ridiculous.

DAUGHTER

Exactly. Laughable. Ha bleedin' ha.

MOTHER

I think myself that was part of it.

FATHER

You're just looking for a way to blame me.

MOTHER

What did O'Hagan have to say for himself? I don't like that man.

FATHER

The latest round of tests are inconclusive. That was the word.

MOTHER

What does that mean?

FATHER

I suppose it means he—they—the team—have come to no conclusions.

MOTHER

He keeps talking about the team—like this is some kind of football match.

DAUGHTER

Spot the ball.

MOTHER

What about the new tests?

FATHER

They're none the wiser. The results are pretty much the same as the last batch. We just have to wait and see.

MOTHER

It's over a week. Surely they can tell us something? Either way.

DAUGHTER

No news may not be good news for me. Trigger happy ... so by analogy plug-pull happy. But isn't that what I wanted?

I'm so tired.

FATHER

He said we shouldn't get our hopes up.

MOTHER

But how long can this go on?

FATHER

He refused to speculate. He did say that she's stable. Still stable. There's been no change in the week. You know what they're like.

MOTHER

No. As a matter of fact I don't know what they're like. How could I know what they're like. You wouldn't let me come to the bloody meeting today.

FATHER

Now hold on a minute. That was all agreed.

MOTHER

It was a fait accompli.

FATHER

I didn't think it appropriate for you to meet the consultant with drink on you. Will you cop on to yourself. How seriously are they going to take you? Now.

DAUGHTER

Now. We're sparking again. Energy eddying around me. Or so it seems. Can I feel the tension or am I still only hearing it?

MOTHER

Please go back to O'Hagan.

FATHER

If she does pull through she could be left as a vegetable.

DAUGHTER

Fuck O'Hagan. What can he know?

MOTHER

A vegetable. Don't say that.

FATHER

It has to be faced. You're not helping one bit here. You're doing a good imitation of an ostrich and to be honest ....

DAUGHTER

To be brutally frank as it were.

FATHER

Look. He didn't hold out much hope, one way or the other.

MOTHER

She was always a fighter. She'll fight.

FATHER

I don't know. Will she? She wanted to die.

MOTHER

I still think it was an accident. A cry for help.

FATHER

It was a serious attempt. She didn't expect anyone home. She wouldn't have been found but we came back early. We have to face that reality.

MOTHER

It just doesn't add up. She had everything to live for.

FATHER

She didn't think so.

MOTHER

Good job. Good prospects. She was a teacher, for godsake.

DAUGHTER

Prospects. What are they? Prospects.

FATHER

Nobody can answer the question why?

MOTHER

She can answer it.

FATHER

Will you look! Look! The evidence of your own eyes, for the love of god.

DAUGHTER

Why? All seems vague now. Must have been a good idea at the time. Must have been ... compelling? Must have been ... urgent? Could I have helped myself? As in—She couldn't help herself. Yes! Exactly. Why did I kill myself? I couldn't help myself.

Is that profound? It feels like a revelation. I couldn't help myself. To be honest, to myself at least. Not much prospect of being honest to anyone else just now. I can't remember why. There is no good reason I can come up with. I was depressed. I went to the doc. I was sad, to be accurate. Not depresssed.

Sad. It's not really a word doctors deal in though. Depressed relaxes them. Sad makes them think you're an eejit—especially when there's no reason for it. I'm sad, doc. Sad about what? Sad about the world; the state it's in. Well, tough.

One in six people presenting at doctors' surgeries are on some kind of antidepressant. Either when they go in or when they come out. Now there's a fact.

So I went in sad and came out on Seroxat. Doctor, I said, I've heard of this stuff. Is it true that one of its side effects is suicidal feelings? Tendencies? No no no no. Ho ho ho ho. No no no no.

I was sad. For years I was sad. Maybe I should just have got used to it. The world is a sad place, after all. But I felt if I could just shift sideways a bit, just shake off some veil over my eyes, just look at the world clear eyed, behold its true nature—I would be in a state of bliss. That the sadness was infinitesimally close to absolute joy. Both sides of the one coin, as it were, and if I could flip the coin I'd be rapturously happy.

I took the tablets. Nothing changed. I was no happier. No sadder. For a few weeks. Then ... Then everything went to hell in a handbasket. The world unravelled.

You know those stories from earthquake zones about solid earth liquifying? It's called liquefaction. Funny, that's a line from an old poem ... *When in silks my Julia goes, The liquefaction of her clothes.* Hmm. I think that's it. It must be a different liquefaction. No. It's the same. The silk turns to liquid. Beautiful.

My liquefaction was of the earthquake variety. That's what happened. Where once there was solid earth, there was nowhere anymore to make a stand. Nothing was reliable. Friends. All? All four of them? I thought they despised me.

Work? A joke. I mispronounced a black kid's name, in third year, a new kid from Ghana. I just read it wrong the first time and it must have got stuck in my head. Adekunle. Andekunle, I called him for a few days. It was just the excuse the class was looking for. Nazi. That was the least of their taunts. I even apologised to Adekunle in front of the class. But that only made it worse. I hated going in. Funny thing was Andy became Adekunle's nickname. I stopped going in.

MOTHER
I just think of her on her own. How desperate she must have been.

FATHER
I do, too. How lonely she must have been.

DAUGHTER
Desperate? Lonely? No. Sad.

MOTHER
If I had only kept in touch more. I don't know why we got so far apart.

DAUGHTER
Drifted. We just drifted.

That's what it feels like now. I'm in a current and it will carry me wherever it's meant to carry me. There's something comforting about it.

FATHER

I keep thinking if we'd got home even a halfhour earlier we'd have found her and saved her. Or the morning we were leaving. We were heading for a seven o'clock flight so we were up at the crack and she came down to say goodbye. She looked bad alright. Trembly and frightened. But sure that's in retrospect. I was just worried about travel stuff. *Reise angst.*

MOTHER

You just don't expect it. I mean I knew we didn't have a perfect relationship. I mean we could have seen more of each other. I thought there was loads of time. I thought it was always about to happen.

DAUGHTER

O stop. Ma. Da. Stop torturing yourselves. You'll break my heart.

MOTHER

We have to have hope.

FATHER

Reading between the lines .... O'Hagan told me that cases like this ... well, it often ends, well, sometimes it's a mercy, he said, for the families; sometimes, the end is an infection. Pneumonia most often.

DAUGHTER

Mercy. Shine thine eyes of mercy towards us. Where's that from? A prayer? Paraclete? Something about a paraclete. Whatever a paraclete is.

Suppose I've to lie here for the rest of my natural. Have I thought about that? Put that in my pipe? They'd stop visiting after a while. There'd be nothing. The odd nurse. Orderly.

94

Totally at their mercy. I won't think like that. I won't think that thought.

That's new. The mind watching the mind. I can say no—I won't think that particular thought. I'll leave it here at the side. I'll park it, as the Americans say. I'll park that thought and come back to it when I'm ready.

MOTHER

In her note she said—This is a vale of tears. And then there was all that stuff about how sorry she was for the pain she'd cause us—but then she said, wrote, "The chestnuts will have their last unleaving". What in god's name does that mean, can you tell me? Hm? "The chestnuts will have their last unleaving. Their mysteries will be lost with them."

FATHER

I don't know. It's a puzzle. She wasn't herself writing that note.

MOTHER

Of course she was herself! We have to respect her.

FATHER

Hold your fire. I meant no disrespect. I don't know what it means. Look. All I'm saying is she was sick. She was suicidal. That's sick alright. In anybody's book. Trees obviously have some major significance that's lost on us.

DAUGHTER

Not trees. Chestnuts. Specific.

MOTHER

Was it anything to do with conkers, do you think? You know this time of year.

FATHER

You'd addle your mind trying to work it out. She must have been very disturbed. She wasn't in her right mind at all. This is what we have to remember. We mustn't forget this. We look at it with our sane minds—ah now you can put that look away: our relatively sane minds, okay? It'll never make sense.

DAUGHTER

It was the little grove of chestnuts on the way to the DART. The ones tucked into that triangular piece of ground near the football pitch. They're the same age as me. So you said, Da. They were planted the year I was born. You used tell me when I was a child that they were planted in my honour. I loved those chestnuts.

It was a spring morning. I was rushing for the eight-fifteen and I was passing the chestnuts. I saw the bark had been peeled. The bark had been peeled off them. It was like a kick in the belly. I just could not believe it. Ignorance, no doubt. A bunch of kids playing. The bark was lying around the ground beneath. For a mad moment I wanted to stick it back on. Actually picked up a strip and tried to find where it had come from. Madness. I felt skinned myself. Like the skin had been slowly peeled off my frame.

Ever since that morning I felt I was walking in the world with no skin. One big open wound. That I had no protection. And I was watching the trees die. Day after day heading for the DART. I couldn't avoid them. I thought about them all the time. I'd look into the face of a kid and wonder was he, or indeed she, capable of murdering a tree. Even out of ignorance. I felt the kids were cursed. That the spirits of the trees would exact a terrible revenge.

It got me down, as they say. This summer I wasn't that way as much. I didn't have to see the chestnuts. But from the first day back in school they were on my mind. Without their bark they were dying. Every morning I passed them. All their leaves were falling. It would almost pass for a normal autumn fall. But there was no fruit, no shiny conkers nestled in their spiky overcoats, that beautiful brown gleaming in the fallen leaves.

And I knew that next spring there'd be no buds.

FATHER
We should maybe work out some kind of a rota.

MOTHER
What do you mean?

FATHER
Look. O'Hagan thinks, well I'm not sure what he thinks exactly, but he said she was stable. He can't say any more than that, I suppose. But we should try and get some normality back into our lives. Some structure.

MOTHER
Well it's hardly a bloody normal situation.

DAUGHTER
You tell him, Ma.

MOTHER
I don't want her left on her own.

FATHER
Isn't that what I'm saying? A rota would help us plan our time better. We could spread the load. We both need sleep.

DAUGHTER

I was teaching a poem. Hopkins' poem—*Margaret are you grieving, Over goldengrove unleaving.* 'Spring and Fall' the poem's called. I just felt so sad. It's a lovely poem but nobody was interested. I was losing my grip on the class already and it was only September. I knew I wouldn't survive. There was the swastika too on the blackboard the day before. I rubbed it off but I knew I should have got to the bottom of it, made an issue of it. Not doing anything about it was the worst thing I could have done. They had me in a place they could manipulate me.

All this was flashing through my head when I was reading the poem. And when I got to the last line—*It is Margaret you grieve for*—I just started to cry. Great big wracking gulps of tears. The lot. Snots and all. And nothing to wipe them with. Like a great big galoot I stood in front of them slobbering and drooling and they just laughed. At first. Then they fell silent. And then there was an edge of panic. They didn't really know what to do. It was only twenty minutes into the class. They were looking at the clock. They knew that something was seriously wrong. Even Richard—Dickhead as he's known to the rest of them—had the smirk wiped off his face by the waves of grief pouring out of me. They certainly had never come across anything like this before.

And it was Adekunle who took things in hand. He came up with a wad of toilet paper. He'd had a bit of a cold and was snuffling through the last few days. It was his kindness I found hardest of all. There were even more tears now. But I took the tissue and Adekunle helped me outside, well kind of steered me out of the room. He led me to the staff room. Gently, the way you'd chivvy a forlorn child or an idiot. Hush hush, Miss, he kept saying. His lovely accent.

There was only Stokes there, as luck would have it. The old stoner himself. He made me a cup of miso and sent Adekunle back with the word that they could have the rest of the class free if they kept it quiet.

Stokes offered to drive me home himself. But I knew he'd my gang for French next. He got me a cab.

FATHER
Would you not head home for a bit of a kip?

MOTHER
Home?

FATHER
You know you can stay with us as long as you need.

MOTHER
No. I'm grand.

FATHER
Why don't you get the head down here for an hour? Out in the family room.

MOTHER
There's always someone in bits out there. I can't handle it.

FATHER
I'm sorry.

MOTHER
It's alright.

DAUGHTER

I want to send a message of thanks. To Adekunle and Stokes. Funny how pathetically grateful I feel towards them. Like they saved my life. Isn't that a strange thing. Like I owe them an enormous debt of gratitude. How could that be?

MOTHER

I'll just put the chair up against the bed and I can stretch my legs underneath. I'm grand.

FATHER

Yeah well, I'd be careful you're not amputated with all them levers and things.

MOTHER

I'll be fine.

FATHER

I'm going to get something to eat. I can't remember if I'd anything yesterday. Will I get you a drop of soup? A sandwich?

MOTHER

Chicken Tikka, if they have it. And will you get me two cream doughnuts. And a cup of tea. Here.

FATHER

Stop now. I don't want any money.

MOTHER

And a newspaper.

FATHER

Any in particular?

MOTHER

As long as it has the Sudoku.

FATHER

The Sudoku. Right. I think they all have that now.

Look. Anja said she'll come in and sit with her too.

DAUGHTER

The rota. I hope she has a bit of chat. That's the problem with the rota. They'll be on their own. I won't hear a thing. I never thought your ears could be hungry.

MOTHER

Do you think they'll do everything for her? I mean everything possible?

FATHER

What are you on about? Sure isn't she getting the best. And I'll want to know why if she's not. It's not for nothing I've forty years as a trade unionist …

DAUGHTER

… negotiating at the highest levels …

FATHER

…negotiating at the highest levels ….

DAUGHTER

… with government ministers…

FATHER

…with government ministers, captains of industry. She'll get the best. You can rely on that.

MOTHER

It's just that she's a suicide ... case ... victim. They might think she has it coming. Remember that heart guy who wouldn't give people the operation if they didn't give up smoking?

FATHER

Ah no. Ah no. You're way off side.

MOTHER

Will you get me a few smokes?

FATHER

You're going to have to start going outside if you want to smoke.

MOTHER

She can't be left. Not yet.

I'm just worried that they'll say—well, she deserves it. She wants to die and she's not worth saving. They mightn't even think it through or anything. Or even let on to themselves. But somewhere inside themselves, in their heart of hearts, they might believe it, and they'd not work as hard for her, to save her.

FATHER

That's a mad thought. Here. Come here to me.

MOTHER

It'll be over my dead body they'll harm a hair of her head.

FATHER

Shush. Shush. Shush.

MOTHER

I'm alright.

FATHER

I know you are.

MOTHER

I'm grand.

FATHER

Look. I'll get that stuff. I won't be long.

Sound of door opening and closing.

DAUGHTER

Ma? Ma? Are you there, Ma? Ma? Ma?

Ma? Ma?

Ma? Ma? Ma?

Are you there? Ma?

MOTHER:

Now. A bit of music. Will I put on the CD? Do you like that, love? Look at you. You're so peaceful. Like you're having a little nap. And any minute now you'll open your eyes and say: Ma, what are you doing here? Where did you come from? So … serene. Serene. Like a little baby.

Music comes on— 'Dimming of the Day'

— The End —

Printed in the United Kingdom
by Lightning Source UK Ltd.
132755UK00002B/25-111/P